tiny titans

AW YEAH TITA

tiny titans

Sidekickin' It

Art Baltazar & Franco
Writers

Art Baltazar
Artist

Dan DiDio SVP-Executive Editor
Jann Jones Elisabeth V. Gehrlein Editors-original series
Simona Martore Assistant Editor-original series
Georg Brewer VP-Design & DC Direct Creative
Bob Harras Group Editor-Collected Editions
Sean Mackiewicz Editor
Robbin Brosterman Design Director-Books

DC COMICS

Paul Levitz President & Publisher
Richard Bruning SVP-Creative Director
Patrick Caldon EVP-Finance & Operations
Amy Genkins SVP-Business & Legal Affairs
Jim Lee Editorial Director-WildStorm
Gregory Noveck SVP-Creative Affairs
Steve Rotterdam SVP-Sales & Marketing
Cheryl Rubin SVP-Brand Management

Cover by Art Baltazar

TINY TITANS: SIDEKICKIN' IT

DC Comics, 1700 Broadway, New York, NY 10019
A Warner Bros. Entertainment Company
Printed by World Color Press, Inc., St-Romuald, QC, Canada 1/6/10. First Printing.
ISBN: 978-1-4012-2653-4

Fiber used in this product line meets the sourcing requirements of the SFI program. www.sfiprogram.org PWC-SFICOC-260

WASH
WASH
SUDS
SUDS
ROBIN!
CHUGGA CHUGGA
DUDE, NEXT TIME WE SHOULD WASH OUR COSTUMES AT MY HOUSE.
ART BALTAZAR
PET CLUB AT WAYNE MANOR

tiny titans

WELL, YOU WOULDN'T BE STUCK BETWEEN A ROCK AND A HARD PLACE IF YOU DIDN'T BOTHER ME SO MUCH!

NOT A BOTHER... ...REALLY... OUCH.

ROBIN

STARFIRE

RAVEN

KID FLASH

MISS MARTIAN

KID DEVIL

CASSIE

BEAST BOY

AQUALAD

WONDER GIRL

BUMBLEBEE

CYBORG

ROSE

SPEEDY

tiny titans
"TOUGH COOKIE"
NUTS & STUFF

AW YEAH NUTS

NUTS & STUFF

NUTS & STUFF

NUTS & STUFF

SCRAM!
NUTS & STUFF

NUTS & STUFF

-BLISS!

OFFICE
tiny titans
HI GUYS!
WHERE ARE YOU GOING, BRAINIAC?
UM, MY NAME IS PSIMON, AND I'M GOING TO MY SCIENCE CLUB MEETING!
SCIENCE CLUB? REALLY? WHAT ARE YOU GOING TO DO THERE?
WE WILL BE DISCUSSING THE TOPIC OF ADDING A NEUTRON TO AN ELECTRON THEREFORE MAKING AN ATOM INTO AN ISOTOPE.
WOW! THAT SOUNDS COOL! I LIKE SCIENCE!
ISOTOPES? NEUTRONS? ELECTRONS? SOUNDS LIKE A ROOM FULL OF BRAINIACS TO ME!

C'MON, WONDERGIRL! LET'S GO! IT'LL BE FUN!

SLADE'S OFFICE

OKAY, BUT YOU OWE ME BIG TIME!

LATER...
WELL, HERE WE ARE. SHALL WE?
LET'S DO IT!
CLUB MEETING

WELCOME BACK, BROTHER PSIMON, TO THE BRAINIAC CLUB!
AAHRRG!! A ROOM FULL OF BRAINIACS!
HEAD BANDS
I SEE YOU BROUGHT FRIENDS.
CAN I HAVE ONE OF THOSE COOL HEADBANDS?

—THINKIN'

tiny titans
HAVE A GOOD PET CLUB MEETING, TITANS!
I'M GOING TO THE STORE TO GET ICE FOR THE PENGUINS!

BEHAVE WHILE I'M GONE. AND, DON'T MAKE A MESS.
CAN YOU GET CHIPS, TOO?
YES.
AND, BEAST BOY?
YES SIR?
YOUR ELEPHANT STAYS OUTSIDE.
YES, SIR.

I'LL BE BACK SOON!
BYE, ALFRED!

I'D LIKE TO BRING OUR PET CLUB MEETING TO ORDER!
LET'S WELCOME OUR NEWEST MEMBERS...

CRUMB AND DOT AND THEIR DOG, SPOT, FROM THE ATOM'S FAMILY!
AW YEAH TITANS!
RUFF!

ALSO, AQUALAD HAS A NEW PET FOR OUR MEETING!
THAT'S RIGHT! HIS NAME IS INKY!

HI INKY!

IT'S OKAY, INKY! THEY'RE JUST SAYING HELLO.

WHAT'S WRONG WITH HIM?
WELL, INKY HAS A DEFENSE MECHANISM WHEN HE'S NERVOUS.
REALLY, WHAT IS IT?
KOOCHIE KOOCHIE KOO!

SSPLOOIT!

IT'S THE INK, ISN'T IT?
YEP, HE SQUIRTS IT WHEN HE'S NERVOUS.
IT WORKS MUCH BETTER UNDERWATER.
SOMEBODY GET THAT SQUID A DIAPER.

AW MAN! WHAT A MESS! WE HAVE TO CLEAN UP! ALFRED'S GONNA BE VERY UPSET WHEN HE SEES THIS!
HE'LL BE HOME SOON.
QUICK! TO THE BAT-WASHING MACHINE!
MINUTES LATER...
NOW, WE ADD SOAP AND OUR COSTUMES WILL BE CLEAN IN A JIFFY!

SHAKE SHAKE
POUR
WASH SOAP

SHAKE SHAKE
POUR
AW YEAH SOAP!

SHAKE SHAKE
POUR
WASH SOAP

UM, HOW MUCH SOAP ARE YOU SUPPOSED TO ADD?
JUST A LITTLE MORE!
WASH SOAP

THERE!
WASH SOAP

NOW, WE CLOSE THE LID...
CLOSE

... AND TURN ON THE SWITCH.

PRESS

CHUG CHUG

SLOG

SLOSH

THAR SHE BLOWS!

INCOMING!

SOAP!

to my GOOD FRIEND ALFRED!
DD!

SUDS!

SOAP!

ROBIN!

SSSHHHH

YUP.

SAME BAT-TIME,

SAME BAT-CHANNEL.

HOLY RINSE CYCLE!

tiny titans
IN "A HOT SPOT"
WALK
WALK
WALK
WALK
WALK

HI, RAVEN!
WHERE ARE YOU GOING?
HI, HOTSPOT.

I'M ON MY WAY TO A BIRD SCOUTS MEETING.
COOL! WHO'S YOUR FRIEND?

THIS IS KID DEVIL. I'M WALKING HIM HOME FROM SCHOOL.
HI, KID DEVIL!

AH AH AH...

CHOOO!

WOW!
THAT'S SO COOL! CHECK THIS OUT!
SNIFF

FFOOSH

FFOOSH!

HA HA
HEE HOH!
HI TITANS!
WHATCHA DOING?
HI FLAMEBIRD!
UM, I WAS JUST HEADING TO A BIRD SCOUTS MEETING.
BIRD SCOUTS? WOW! CAN I JOIN?
HMM... FLAME... BIRD...
YES, I SUPPOSE YOU CAN.
OOOHH! ME, ME, ME! HOW ABOUT ME?!!
HOTSPOT? IT'S FOR BIRD PEOPLE ONLY.
YOU'RE NOT A BIRD PERSON...
...YOU'RE A FIRE GUY.

FFOOSH!

OKAY, YOU'RE IN!
BUT WE'RE GONNA HAVE TO GET YOU A FIREPROOF HAT!
-THAT'S HOT!

tiny titans presents the Kroc files in...
HOW TO PICK UP THE DRY CLEANING.
"the RIGHT WAY"
"the Kroc WAY"
DRY DRY DRY DRY
MMMMMM
STOMP!
LAUNDROMAT
-THANK YOU.

tiny titans
BUBBLE SQUARES
EXAMPLE
R
TAKE TURNS DRAWING LINES TO CONNECT ONE BUBBLE TO ANOTHER.
WRITE YOUR INITIALS IN THE BOX WHEN YOU CONNECT FOUR BUBBLES!
THE PERSON WHO MAKES THE MOST BOXES WINS THIS BUBBLE CHALLENGE!

Special bonus Pin-Up!
HAWK
DOVE
RAVEN
FRANCO '08

YOU'RE RIGHT, LAGOON BOY!
MY CEREAL IS STILL CRUNCHY!
BREAKFAST UNDERWATER ROCKS!
TOLD YA.
NEXT TIME WE'LL TRY THE PANCAKES!
AQUA-OH'S
ART BALTAZAR 200
AW YEAH TITANS!

tiny titans

OKAY, BRAINIAC! TELL ME WHERE THEY'RE HIDING!

WE'RE JUST PLAYING HIDE-N-SEEK. ARE YOU SURE THIS IS FAIR?

CASSIE

KID DEVIL

PLASMUS

SHIMMER

GIZMO

PSIMON

AQUALAD

CYBORG

STARFIRE

RAVEN

KID FLASH

MISS MARTIAN

MAMMOTH

TERRA

BEAST BOY

ROBIN

WONDER GIRL

BUMBLEBEE

JERICHO

ROSE

SPEEDY

AW YEAH TITANS!
WELCOME TO OUR FIRST OFFICIAL MEETING OF PET CLUB PARADISE ISLAND!
tiny titans
I'D LIKE TO INTRODUCE OUR NEWEST MEMBERS! MY COUSIN, CASSIE AND HER PET CYCLOPS,
CECELIA!
AW YEAH CASSIE!
AW YEAH CECELIA!
UM, WONDER GIRL, I COULDN'T BRING THE CYCLOPS.
WHY NOT?
HER MOM SAID NO. SHE HAD HOMEWORK.
SO, I BROUGHT YOONI THE UNICORN INSTEAD.

OKAY! LET'S ALL WELCOME YOONI the UNICORN!
AW YEAH YOONI!
AND I BROUGHT MY PET MATILDA THE MINOTAUR!
AW YEAH MATILDA!

I REALLY LIKE YOUR DRESS.
MOO.
LET'S ALSO WELCOME OUR GUESTS STARFIRE AND BUMBLEBEE!
AW YEAH STAR!
AW YEAH BEE!

BECAUSE NO BOYS ARE ALLOWED TO TOUCH THE GROUND HERE IN PARADISE ISLAND.
GIRLS ONLY!
BUT...
NO BUTS!
YOU'RE LUCKY MY MOM SAID YOU COULD COME AT ALL!

WELL, WHY IS FLUFFY ON THE GROUND?

HE'S NOT TOUCHING THE GROUND...
...HE'S IN A FISHBOWL.
SO TECHNICALLY, HE'S IN THE WATER.

WELL THEN, HOW COME ELIZABETH ISN'T ON THE TABLE?

BECAUSE SHE'S A GIRL!

UM... HELLO... UM... ELIZABETH IS A GIRL'S NAME!

WELL, I DIDN'T KNOW. I THOUGHT SHE WAS A MAMMAL.
SHE IS A MAMMAL. MAMMALS CAN BE GIRLS TOO.
I'M NOT A MAMMAL.

YOU'RE NOT?
WHY ISN'T LAGOON BOY A MAMMAL?
`CAUSE HE LIVES UNDERWATER.

WHAT?!

I'M CONFUSED AND I DON'T EVEN HAVE A PET!
SUDDENLY...
OKAY, BOYS! TIME'S UP!
TIME TO GET YOU BACK TO THE TREEHOUSE!
WONDER WOMAN!

GREAT! ANOTHER PET CLUB MEETING WHERE WE GET NOTHING ACCOMPLISHED.

WHAT DO YOU MEAN?

WE JUST FOUND OUT LAGOON BOY'S NOT A MAMMAL!

OH, RIGHT.

WOOSH!

SORRY, LET'S STOP TALKING ABOUT THE FISHBOY.

I'M NOT A FISH!

WELL, YOU'RE NOT A LAGOON, EITHER.

OH, GREAT HERA!

—WONDERFUL!

LET ME INTRODUCE TO YOU THE SUPER CYBORG VACUUM CLEANER SPECIAL 3000!

WOW, CYBORG! THAT THING MOVES REALLY FAST!
MMMMMMM
LOOKS LIKE IT'S DOING A GOOD JOB CLEANING, TOO!
MMMMMMMM
YEP! AND I HAVE FULL CONTROL RIGHT AT MY FINGERTIPS!
MMMMMM

THAT'S GREAT, CYBORG! CAN IT MAKE BREAKFAST OR DO LAUNDRY?
OR MAKE HOT WINGS?
MMMMM

AAHH!
MY CAPE!
MMMMM
IT ATE MY CAPE!
WELL, IT IS BREAKFAST TIME.
MMMMM

URK!

HEY!

GIMME BACK MY JUMPROPE!

AAH!

MMMMMMM

WILDEBEESTE! STOP THAT VACUUM CLEANER!

BLAH!

MMM
MMM

HEY!
WAIT!
STOP!

BRUSH
BRUSH

MAN, I HEAR YA, WILLIE.
SOMETIMES A REGULAR TOOTHBRUSH JUST DOESN'T CUT IT!

-FLOSS TOO.

tiny titans

BEE BEE!

B.[B.]?

UM, DID YOU JUST CALL ME "B.B." AS IN BEAST BOY?

FFBBTT!

OH YEAH?
HA HA HA
POP!
BLAH!
STRETCH!
FFFBBTT!
POP!
STRETCH!
FFFBBTT!

—AWWW!♥

MEANWHILE ON PARADISE ISLAND...
tiny titans
IN
"STAY FOR DINNER"
MAN, I REALLY MISSED CECELIA AT THE PET CLUB MEETING TODAY!
YEAH, ME TOO! I WONDER IF SHE EVER FINISHED HER HOMEWORK?
LET'S GO SEE HER!

MINUTES LATER...
DING DONG!

HELLO, MRS. CYCLOPS!
OOH! HELLO GIRLS! MMMM, GOOD TO SEE YOU.
IS CECE HOME?
SHE SURE IS.
C'MON IN.

SHAKE
SHAKE
SHAKE
HOW TO COOK TITANS
OH, DON'T WORRY, IT'S A CYCLOPS FAMILY TRADITION. WE SPRINKLE SALT ON ALL OUR GUESTS.
SALT?

WOULD YOU LIKE SOME STUFFING?... OH, I MEAN ... BREAD?
YOU GIRLS LOOK A LITTLE THIN.
SHAKE
SHAKE
SHAKE
MORE SALT?
NOPE. ACTUALLY, IT'S PEPPER.
ACHOO!
HEY, CECE, CAN YOU COME OUT AND PLAY?
I CAN'T GO YET. MY MOM TOLD ME TO KEEP AN EYE ON MY HOMEWORK!
ARE YOU STAYING FOR DINNER, GIRLS?
I THINK SHE HAS HER EYE ON US TOO.
EYE-YIE-YIE!

tiny titans PRESENTS... the Kroc files IN...

"HOW TO BAKE A CHOCOLATE CAKE."

"the RIGHT WAY"
ADD THE CHOCOLATE...
CHOCOLATE MIX

MIX IN THE EGGS...

BAKE FOR TWENTY MINUTES.

"THE Kroc WAY"
ADD THE CHOCOLATE.
CHEW
CHEW

MIX IN THE EGGS...
RUN RUN
CHICKEN COOP

BAKE FOR TWENTY MINUTES...
BAWK
BAWK
CLUCK
CHICKEN COOP
CACKLE
CLUCK
BAWK
SHAKE
SHAKE
RATTLE

WAA-LAH! ENJOY!
CHICKEN COOP
THANK YOU!

TIME for JOKES
HEY SPEEDY!
HI, ENIGMA.
WANNA HEAR A JOKE?
NOT REALLY.
OKAY! WHAT DO YOU CALL A CAMEL WITH NO HUMPS?
WHAT?
HUMPHREY!
WHY DID THE ROOSTER CROSS THE ROAD?
WHY?
BECAUSE THE CHICKEN WAS ON VACATION!
WHY DO COWS WEAR BELLS AROUND THEIR NECKS?
BECAUSE THEIR HORNS DON'T WORK!
HOW DO MONSTERS COUNT TO ONE HUNDRED?
ON THEIR FINGERS AND TOES?
AAHHH!!!

PARADISE ISLAND PET CLUB PIN-UP!
AW YEAH TITANS!
CECELIA
YOONI
MATILDA
CASSIE
WONDER GIRL
ART BALTAZAR 2009!

BUNNIES!
I GUESS ZATARA SAID THE WRONG MAGIC WORD AGAIN, HUH?
WELL, AT LEAST HE DIDN'T TURN US INTO MONKEYS.
ART BALTAZAR 2008
BUNNIES, BUNNIES, EVERYWHERE BUNNIES!

tiny titans

OH, C'MON, TERRA.
YOU'RE NOT EVEN TRYING.
SCULPT

CASSIE
KID DEVIL
PLASMUS
SHIMMER
GIZMO
PSIMON
AQUALAD
CYBORG
STARFIRE
RAVEN
KID FLASH
MISS MARTIAN
MAMMOTH
TERRA
BEAST BOY
ROBIN
WONDER GIRL
BUMBLEBEE
JERICHO
ROSE
SPEEDY

MEANWHILE, AT WAYNE MANOR...
tiny titans
AW YEAH PET CLUB!

LISTEN UP, TITANS! BEFORE YOU TALK ABOUT YOUR PET CLUB MEETING, LET ME REMIND YOU...
BUT, ALFRED, THE NUMBER ONE RULE OF PET CLUB IS WE DON'T TALK ABOUT PET CLUB.

I WILL BE SITTING IN ON THIS ONE.

THE LAST TIME I LEFT YOU ALONE FOR YOUR PET CLUB MEETING, YOU FLOODED THE HOUSE WITH BUBBLES.
HEE HEE

NOT FUNNY.
SORRY.

SO THIS TIME, I ALREADY WASHED THE LAUNDRY.

...AND I DID ALL THE GROCERY SHOPPING.
MMM... CARROTS!

AND I PREPARED MY HOT CUP OF TEA!

SIP!

SO, UNDER MY SUPERVISION...
...YOU MAY CONTINUE YOUR MEETING.

AW YEAH PET CLUB!

LET'S CALL OUR MEETING TO ORDER.
OH, PLEASE DON'T DO THAT AGAIN.

FIRST OFF, LET'S ALL WELCOME BACK SUPERGIRL TO PET CLUB!
AW YEAH SUPERGIRL!

I BROUGHT ALL MY SUPER PETS THIS TIME! I HOPE IT'S OKAY.
OH, THAT'S SUPER.
SUPER DUPER SUPER.
POP

NEXT, LET'S WELCOME OUR NEWEST MEMBER ZATARA AND HIS PET BUNNY ABBY!
AW YEAH ZATARA!
AW YEAH ABBY!

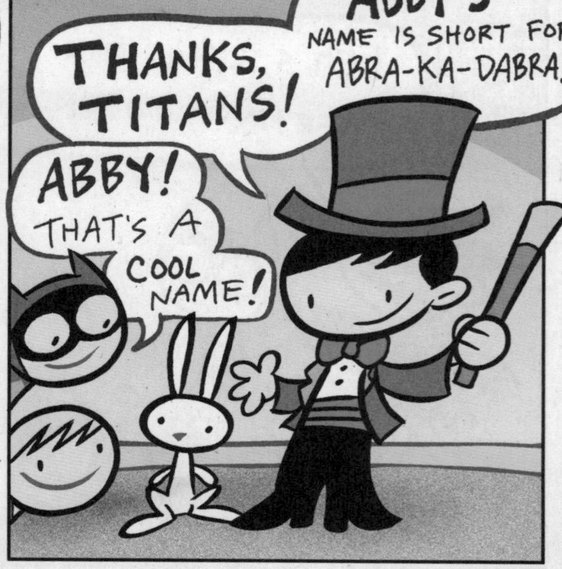
THANKS, TITANS!
ABBY'S NAME IS SHORT FOR ABRA-KA-DABRA!
ABBY! THAT'S A COOL NAME!

OOH! I REALLY LIKE YOUR HAT! IS IT MAGIC?
IT SURE IS.
CAN WE TRY IT?
WELL, UM, IT'S NOT REALLY A TOY. REMEMBER WHAT HAPPENED LAST TIME?
WHEN BEPPO GOT AHOLD OF MY MAGIC WAND?
YEP, WE WERE ALL TURNED INTO MONKEYS!
OH, C'MON. IT WASN'T THAT BAD!
POP
LOOK! YOUR BUNNY ABBY IS GETTING ALONG NICELY WITH THE SUPER PETS!
SLAP!
EEP!

MMMRROOWW!!

AH! LOOK OUT!
STREAKY, STOP!
MMRROOW
POP!
ARF
ARF
BUMP
AHK! MY HAT!
BOP!

AHK! MY WAND!

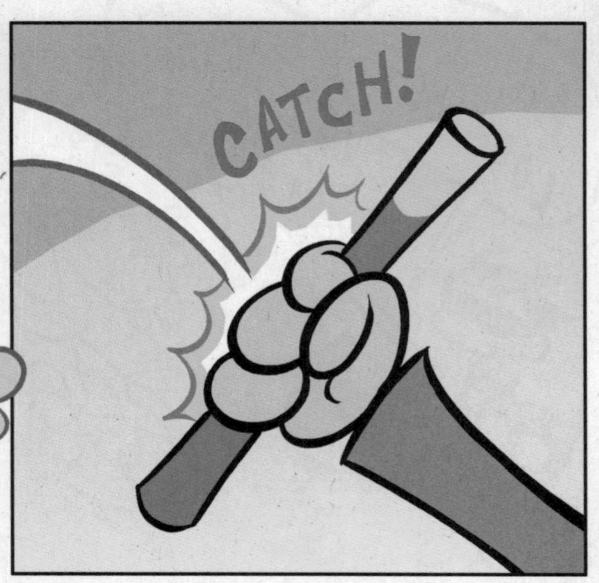
CATCH!

JUMP!

WHEW!

UH, OH!
NOW, BEPPO, LET'S THINK ABOUT THIS...

No, No, No!
TAP!
KA-BUNNY!

WELL, AT LEAST I BOUGHT PLENTY OF CARROTS.
HEY! WHY IS THIS ONE BROWN?
SECONDS LATER...
DUDE, OUR WAYNE MANOR PET CLUB MEETINGS ALWAYS SEEM TO END LIKE THIS.
WITH BUNNIES?
BUNNIES, PENGUINS, BUBBLES. IT'S ALL THE SAME THING.
POP
HEY, WE GOT ANY MORE OF THOSE CARROTS?

tiny titans
AW YEAH TITANS! WHAT ARE YA WATCHING?
THE SUPER HERO DVD SUPER SPECIAL BOX SET!
COOL, CAN I WATCH TOO?
SURE! WAIT, NO YOU CAN'T.
WHY NOT?
IT'S YOUR TURN TO WATCH THE TINY TERROR TITANS.
OH.
LATER...
WELL, ROSE, THESE ARE THE TINY TERROR TITANS.
BABIES?
WELL, THEY'RE TODDLERS.
YOU KEEP THEM IN A CAGE?
IT'S A PLAYPEN. WE DON'T CALL 'EM TERRORS FOR NOTHING.
LI'L DISRUPTOR
DREADBOLT
MISS PERSUADER
COPPERHEAD

GOOD LUCK.

SO, UH, **HI!**
MY **NAME** IS **ROSE.**

HI, ROSE!
ROSIE!
ROSE!
BOO BOO.

HEY, WANNA **SEE** WHAT'S UNDER MY EYEPATCH?
YES.
YES.
YEAH.
WOOO.

AAHH!!!

WHAT? IT'S JUST MY EYE!
EYE!
I SEE!
EYE!
EEE OH!
SO, ARE YOU GUYS HUNGRY?
YEP.
YEAH.
YES.
FFWWEE!
WHAT DO YOU WANT TO EAT?
NACHOS.
NACHOS.
NACHOS.
NANA!
NACHOS IT IS!
BE RIGHT BACK!

AW YEAH NACHOS!

ROSIE, CAN YOU MAKE THESE HOTTER?
HOTTER?
YEAH, HOTTER!

SURE, I BROUGHT EXTRA HOT SAUCE FOR YOU!
HOT

TRY IT NOW!
HOT
POUR
SQUIRT
SHAKE

NOPE. NOT HOT ENOUGH.
MAKE 'EM HOTTER!

HOTTER!
POUR
POUR
HOT
SHAKE

NOPE, NOT HOT ENOUGH.

THAT SHOULD FINALLY DO IT. I USED UP ALL THE HOT SAUCE!
POUR
POUR
EMPTY

HEY, PSIMON! DO YOU LIKE NACHOS?
OOH YEAH!

HERE, TRY ONE.
WHY, THANK YOU.

– WATER, PLEASE.

tiny titans EPILOGUE...

HOP

to my GOOD FRIEND ALFRED!
DD!
HOP
HOP

HOP
JUMP

SHAZAM!

KA-BOOM!

FFWOOSH!

DING DONG
KNOCK
KNOCK

UM, EXCUSE ME, SIR. BUT DID YOU SEE A LITTLE BROWN BUNNY HERE?

LET'S SEE. WAS HE WEARING A LITTLE CAPE AND LOOKED LIKE A MEMBER OF A PET CLUB?

PET CLUB, SIR?
OH, I'M SORRY. I'M NOT SUPPOSED TO TALK ABOUT PET CLUB.
CHECK BACK NEXT WEEK.

OKAY, SIR. I'LL TRY AGAIN LATER.
YEP.
SEE YA THEN.

YOU NEVER KNOW WHAT COULD HAPPEN AROUND HERE.
FEET OFF THE TABLE, KROC!

MARVELOUS! KOO-KOO-KATCHOO!

PET CLUB MAMMAL TRAVEL

HELP **ROBIN** FIND A PATH TO **LAGOON BOY** BY USING THE CIRCLES WITH **MAMMALS**.

HINT: MAMMALS WILL HAVE HAIR!

ASK FOR HELP IF YOU NEED TO! YOU'RE AWESOME!

AW YEAH BONUS PIN-UP!

RACE YA?
SHOW HER, KID FLASH!
C'MON, SUPERGIRL. YOU CAN BEAT HIM!
ART BALTAZAR 2009!
WHO'S THE FASTEST?!

tiny titans

WANNA RACE?

SPEEDY'S JUST MY NAME, Y'KNOW.

START

CASSIE
KID DEVIL
PLASMUS
SHIMMER
GIZMO
PSIMON
AQUALAD
CYBORG
STARFIRE
RAVEN
KID FLASH
MISS MARTIAN
MAMMOTH
TERRA
BEAST BOY
ROBIN
WONDER GIRL
BUMBLEBEE
JERICHO
ROSE
SPEEDY

LEFT! RIGHT!
LEFT, RIGHT, LEFT!!!
tiny titans
MAN!
COACH LOBO IS CRAZY!
YEAH, WE'VE BEEN RUNNING FOR AN HOUR STRAIGHT!
MOVE IT, TITANS!!
IT'S GOOD EXERCISE FOR YA!
BURN THOSE CALORIES!
SIDEKICK CITY

I CAN'T TAKE IT ANYMORE!
SO... SO... TIRED.
OOFFF!
UNNGH!
AW NO TITANS! WHAT DO YA THINK YER DOING?
SIDEKICK CITY
BUT... BUT... COACH LOBO, WE'RE EXHAUSTED!
WE NEED REST!
THIS AIN'T NO JUICE BAR!
THAT'S THE PROBLEM WITH YOU KIDS TODAY! EVERYTHING'S A VACATION!
BACK ON MY PLANET, WHEN I WAS A KID, I HAD TO RUN TO SCHOOL UPHILL BOTH WAYS!
BOTH WAYS, SIR?
YOU BETCHA BOTH WAYS!
HERE WE GO.

GOOD OL' FASHIONED EXERCISE!

I EXERCISED ALL THE TIME!

HOW DO YA THINK I GOT THESE?

SIDEKICK CITY

SEAFOOD?

YELLOW SUN?

IMPLANTS?

TOXIC CHEMICALS?

KRYPTONIAN RADIATION?

LOTS OF MILK?

PINEAPPLE AND BANANA DIET?

INSECT BITE?
BAD TOOTHPASTE?
HAM SANDWICHES?
TOAD LICKING?
COMIC BOOKS?
EARTH'S GRAVITY?
METEORITES?
THE INTERNET?
PEACH NECTAR?
SIDEKICK
HOT WING SAUCE?
THE GREEN LANTERN CORPS?
RIGHT!
LOTS OF EXERCISE!
SIDEKICK CITY
ATTENTION!!
NOW IT'S TIME TO GET THE SCHOOL INTO SHAPE!
SIDEKICK CITY

MINUTES LATER...
GLAD YOU ALL COULD MAKE IT OUT HERE TODAY.
WELCOME TO THE FIRST DAY OF TINY TITANS FITNESS!
YOU MADE US COME OUT HERE.
I WAS IN THE MIDDLE OF MY SCIENCE PROJECT.
OUR FIRST ASSIGNMENT WILL BE A GLOBAL RACE!
SIDEKICK CITY
GLOBAL?
THAT'S FAR!
AS IN, THE WORLD?
HOW EARTHY.
YES!
A RACE AROUND THE WORLD WILL SURELY GET SIDEKICK CITY ELEMENTARY STUDENTS INTO SHAPE!
OH BOY! THE WORLD!
I LIKE RACES!
BETCHA I'M FASTER!
NO WAY, INERTIA! I RAN AROUND THE WORLD TONS OF TIMES!
NOT FASTER THAN ME!

AW YEAH TITANS! THE FIRST TO CROSS THE FINISH LINE GETS AN "A" IN GYM CLASS!
ON YER MARK!
GET SET!
SIDEKICK CITY
HUH?
I DON'T RUN.
I'LL BE IN THE LIBRARY.

tiny titans
AS THE RACE CONTINUES...
RUN
RUN
RUN
JOG

EERRRTT!
HHMM.
WHAT'S WRONG? WHY'D WE STOP?
WATER.
WATER?

YEP, THE OCEAN'S IN OUR WAY.
UM, ANYBODY HAVE A BOAT?

US FISH GUYS DON'T NEED A BOAT!
THAT'S RIGHT!
I GOT AN EXTRA PAIR OF THESE IF ANYONE NEEDS THEM!
I'LL TAKE 'EM! I GOT MY SHARK SPRAY TOO... JUST IN CASE!
SHARK SPRAY
THEN LET'S GO, TITANS!
LAST ONE IN IS A JELLY FISH!
DANG! I FORGOT THE JELLYFISH SPRAY!
POP
POP

–AW YEAH FLYIN'

ONE CUP OF YOUR HOUSE BLEND, MY GOOD MAN!
ANYTHING ELSE, SIR?
NOPE. I HAVE ENOUGH TIME TO ENJOY A CUP WHILE MY STUDENTS RACE AROUND THE WORLD.
tiny titans
SIDEKICK CITY

AH! TIME TO CATCH UP ON MY CAPTAIN MARVEL!

OH SHAZAM!

COMICS!

tiny titans
MEANWHILE, IN A BIG CITY, THE RACE CONTINUES...
RUN
TROT
RACE
RUN
JOG

HI, SHELLY!
HI, CASSIE!
I REALLY LIKE THAT OUTFIT!

THANK YOU!
JEANS AND A T-SHIRT MAKE A PERFECT COSTUME!
HOW ABOUT IT?!

WHAT ARE YOU DOING, CASSIE?
WE HAVE A RACE TO FINISH!
I'M JUST TALKING TO MY FRIEND SHELLY.
NICE TO MEET YOU, SHELLY.
OOH, SHELLY! YOU ARE SOOOO SHINY!
WOW! YOU'RE JUST LIKE A MIRROR!
WE CAN SEE OURSELVES IN YOUR FACE!
THANKS TITANS!
WHEN I LOOK IN THE MIRROR IT LOOKS BACK AT ME AND LOOKS BACK AT ME AND LOOKS BACK AT ME AND LOOKS BACK AT ME AND LOOKS BACK AT ME AND LOOKS BACK AT ME AND LOOKS BACK AT ME AND LOOKS BACK AT ME AND LOOKS BACK...
PRETTY PRETTY!

...AND LOOKS BACK AT ME!

MEANWHILE, IN THE DESERT...

¿QUE ES ÉSTO, **MAS**?

NO SÉ, **MENOS**. ¡VAMOS A SÉGUIRLOS!

AY SÍ TITANS!
¿A DÓNDE VAS CON TANTA PRISA?
HUH?
WE'RE RACING AROUND THE WORLD.
¿PODREMOS ACOMPAÑARLOS?
SURE.

WELL! THE WINNER SHOULD BE CROSSING THAT FINISH LINE ANY MINUTE NOW!
FINISH!
FLY
RUN
RUN
WET
SPLASH

FINISH!

SIDEKICK CITY LIBRARY
BIRDS

FINISH
BIRDS

AND THE WINNER IS...
FINISH

BUMP!
FINISH
RUN RUN
JOG
SKIP
RUN
TRAMPLE
TROT
RUN
RUN

?
RAVEN.
FINISH

RAVEN!
RAVEN!
RAVEN!
WAS THERE EVER ANY DOUBT?
RAVEN!
RAVEN!
RAVEN!

—RAVEN!

tiny titans
"ONE MORE CONTEST"

HI, ATOM!
HELLO, MRS. ATOM. HI, SMIDGEN!
HI, MOLECULE!
HELLO, MOLECULE.

MAN, IT SURE IS FUN BEING TINY!
IT'S AWESOME!
REAL, REAL AWESOME!

AW YEAH TINY TINY TITANS!

I BETCHA I CAN SHRINK TINIER THAN YOU.

YOU DO?
YEP!
OKAY, GO!

SHRINK!
SHRINK!

DA-DA!

SHRINK!

OH C'MON! NO FAIR!

SORRY, MOLECULE.
NO MATTER HOW SMALL WE GET...
...SMIDGEN IS ALWAYS SMALLER!
NEXT TIME WE'RE STICKING TO THE "NO BABY" RULE!

—LITTLE BIT!

tiny titans COIN RACE!
FINISH LINE!
FLIP A COIN.
IF IT LANDS ON HEADS
MOVE SUPERGIRL AHEAD
ONE SPACE.
IF IT LANDS ON TAILS
MOVE KID FLASH AHEAD
ONE SPACE.
KEEP GOING
UNTIL
THERE'S A
WINNER!
START

AW YEAH PIN-UP!

RAVEN, ARE YOU SURE THIS IS HOMEWORK?
IT MUST BE EXTRA CREDIT!
ART BALTAZAR 2009
RAVEN'S BOOK OF MAGIC SPELLS

HAPPY BIRTHDAY

NO CLOWNS

SORRY, DUELA.

THERE'S A STRICT "NO CLOWNS POLICY" AT THIS PARTY.

CASSIE

KID DEVIL

PLASMUS

SHIMMER

GIZMO

PSIMON

AQUALAD

CYBORG

STARFIRE

RAVEN

KID FLASH

MISS MARTIAN

MAMMOTH

TERRA

BEAST BOY

ROBIN

WONDER GIRL

BUMBLEBEE

JERICHO

ROSE

SPEEDY

tiny titans
"MIXIN' IT UP"

AW YEAH TITANS! WANNA HAVE SOME FUN?

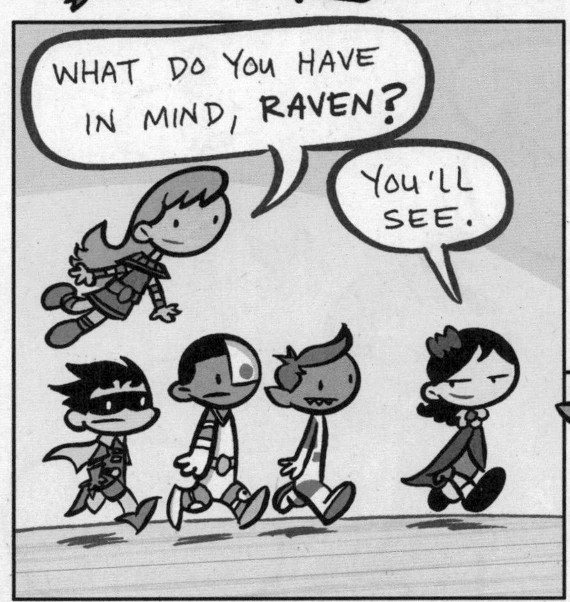
WHAT DO YOU HAVE IN MIND, RAVEN?
YOU'LL SEE.

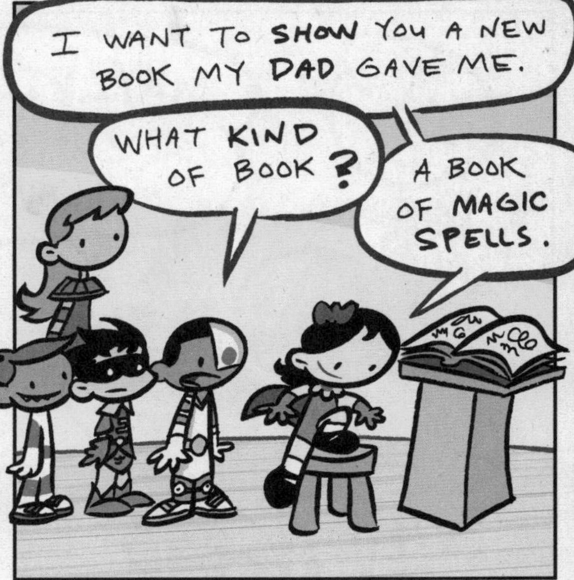
I WANT TO SHOW YOU A NEW BOOK MY DAD GAVE ME.
WHAT KIND OF BOOK?
A BOOK OF MAGIC SPELLS.

AZARATH, METRION, ZINTHOS!

POP
WHO DARES TO SUMMON ME?
THE MIGHTY MR. MXYZPTLK?

MXYZPTLK? THE SUPERMAN VILLAIN?
YEAH! I LOVE THIS GUY!

CHILDREN? DON'T YOU KNOW SUCH MISCHIEF WILL CAUSE ME TO WREAK HAVOC UPON YOU?

PREPARE YOURSELVES, YOUNG ONES! YOU WILL FEEL THE MAGIC OF...

HEY! MY HAT! YOU CAN'T TAKE MY HAT!
YOINK!

GIVE IT BACK, SHORTY!

SHORTY? YOU'RE SHORTER THAN US, YA BIG DORK!
I AM NOT A DORK!
I AM AN IMP!

UM...

IMP? I'M NOT SURE WE SHOULD BE SAYING THAT.
YEAH, IT SOUNDS LIKE A BAD WORD.
IT'S NOT A BAD WORD!
I AM AN IMP!
ARE YOU SURE YOU'RE NOT AN ELF?
OR A LEPRECHAUN?
NO, NO, NO!
I AM AN IMP!
NOW GIVE ME BACK MY HAT!
ALL RIGHT! HERE'S YOUR HAT, YA BIG BABY! IT DOESN'T MATCH ME ANYWAY!
I AM NOT A BABY!
I AM NOT AN ELF!
I AM MR. MXYZPTLK, THE MIGHTY IMP!

ARE YOU SURE?

AZARATH, METRION, ZINTHOS!

FFFZZZZ

HUH? WHO DARES SUMMON THE MIGHTY BAT-MITE?
POP
YEAH!
THAT'S AN IMP!

HE'S EVEN SMALLER THAN YOU, MXY!
HA HA HEE HOH!

THEY'RE RIGHT. I AM SMALLER.
OH KLTPZYXM!
?
POOF!

WHAT HAPPENED? WHERE'D HE GO?
MXY SAID HIS NAME BACKWARDS THEN DISAPPEARED!
REALLY? BRING HIM BACK! I MISS HIM!
ALL RIGHT!

AZARATH METRION ZINTHOS!

POP!

KLTPZYXM!

POOF!

AZARATH, METRION, ZINTHOS!

APPEAR!

KLTPZYXM!

POOF!

RAVEN! I REALLY LIKE YOUR COOL NEW STYLIN' IMP FASHION!
REALLY? HERE, STAR, YOU CAN HAVE THE HAT.
THE COLORS MATCH YOUR OUTFIT PERFECTLY!
I'LL GET ANOTHER ONE TOMORROW!

-POOF!

tiny titans
"BATTLE FOR THE COW."

HEY, WHAT ARE YOU GUYS DOING?

THAT COW HAS BATMAN'S CAPE AND COWL.
ALFRED SAID WE CAN'T COME BACK TO WAYNE MANOR UNTIL WE GET BATMAN'S STUFF BACK.

WELL, HOW DID...?
YOU DON'T WANNA KNOW.

WELL, WHY DON'T YOU JUST...?
WE TRIED THAT ALREADY.

NO PROBLEM! I GOT THIS!

NEVER FEAR! Super BEAST BOY IS HERE!

WATCH THIS, GENTLEMEN!

HI THERE, MR. COW! I'M GONNA TAKE THAT CAPE AND COWL BACK NOW.

MMOOO
CRASH!
MOO

THAT'S IT!

IT'S A BATTLE FOR THE COWL!

MOO
CRASH
BAM MOO

I GOT IT! I GOT IT!
DUDE, THAT'S YOUR CAPE.

HI, BOYS! WHAT ARE YOU DOING?

STARFIRE! LOOK AT THE PRETTY COW!
OOH! LET'S GO SAY HI!

WAIT! NO!
DON'T GO OVER THERE!

WHAT A SWEET COW.
HERE'S YOUR CAPE.
C'MON, BOYS... ...IT'S LUNCHTIME AND ALFRED'S MAKING SOUP.
—MOO!

HAPPY BIRTHDAY TO ROBIN! HAPPY BIRTHDAY TO YOU!
tiny titans

PRESENTS! PRESENTS! PRESENTS! PRESENTS! PRESENTS!

HERE, ROBIN!
OPEN OUR PRESENT FIRST!
HEE HEE!
THANKS, GIRLS.

WOW! A NEW COSTUME! THANKS!

HERE! OPEN MINE!

ANOTHER COSTUME? THANKS.

HERE! OPEN MINE!

ANOTHER COSTUME? UM... WHAT ARE YOU GUYS TRYING TO SAY?

MAYBE IT'S TIME FOR A CHANGE.
MAYBE YOU SHOULD BE NIGHTWING AGAIN.
YEAH, ICEBUCKET! GIVE IT A TRY!
YA NEED TO DITCH THE FISH-SCALED UNDERWEAR AND ELF SHOES, DUDE.
BUT, I LIKE THE FISH SCALES.
to my Good
TRY THEM ON!
ALL OF THEM?
YEAH!
OKAY.
MINUTES LATER...
WHAT DO YOU THINK?
GREY? I DON'T KNOW.
TRY THE NEXT ONE!
NOT BAD. TOO EARTH TWO-ISH.
TRY THE NEXT ONE!
NICE. I'M KINDA DIGGIN' THE NINJA SHOES.
NEXT!

THIS IS PRETTY COOL.
BUT IT NEEDS SOME GREEN.
NEXT ONE!
BOOTS AND PANTS!
HHMM... QUITE REFRESHING!
NEXT!
A RUBBER SUIT?
NO THANKS. IT'S A BIT SNUG.
I FEEL LIKE I'M IN A MOVIE.
NEXT!
DON'T FORGET THE DETACHABLE PONYTAIL!
YEAH, I GOT IT.
NEXT!
I KINDA LIKE THIS ONE!
NEXT!
C'MON, GUYS. A WIG AND GOGGLES?
UM... NO.
NEXT!
AW YEAH ROBIN!
PERFECT!
THAT CHICKEN OUTFIT ROCKS!
COOL!
CLUCK CLUCK
HA HA
LOVE THE COOL KNIGHT'S WINGS CAPE!
KNIGHT'S WINGS
IT'S HOT JUST LIKE THEIR CHICKEN WINGS!
SUDDENLY, YOUR GREEN UNDERWEAR AND ELF SHOES DON'T LOOK SO BAD, HUH, ICEBUCKET?
SOMEONE CALL THE COMMISSIONER!
-CHICKEN!

tiny tiny titans
IN "SHOP SHRINKING"
OH MY!
WHAT A BEAUTIFUL DRESS!

OH NO!
THIS DRESS IS TWO SIZES TOO SMALL!
WHAT'S A GIRL TO DO?

SHRINK A LITTLE, MAMA!
OH RIGHT!

PERFECT FIT!

-SHOPPIN

tiny titans
HEY, WHAT'S CONTINUITY?

CONTINUITY?
IT'S THE CONSISTENCY OF CONTIGUOUS EVENTS, STORIES, CHARACTERS, PLOTS, AND PLACES SET IN THE DC UNIVERSE OBSERVED BY THE COMIC READER.

ARE E IN CONT UITY?
I DON'T THINK SO. WE'RE SIDEKICKS.
I'M IN CONTINUITY!

YOU ARE?
AW YEAH TITANS! I'M A SUPER HERO!
THAT'S AWESOME!
SUPERMAN

HEY TITANS! IT'S TIME TO GO TO THE SIDEKICK PICNIC!

OOH! CAN I GO?!

SORRY DUDE, SIDEKICKS ONLY.
ANYWAY, IT'S NOT IN YOUR CONTINUITY.
BUT I'M A SUPERHERO!
EXACTLY!

—ONGOING!

tiny titans presents the Kroc files IN: "WALKING IN THE RAIN."

"THE RIGHT WAY"

WALK
WALK

the RETURN OF THE BAT-COW!
SEE? WHAT DID I TELL YA?
SPECIAL BONUS PIN-UP!
ART BALTAZAR 2009

OUR PRINCIPAL
Welcome to DETENTION
HHMM...
GUM
ZZZZ.
HI, ROBBIE!
IT'S ALL YOUR FAULT, WONDER NERD!
ART BALTAZAR 2009
UNGH!
INFINITE DETENTION

tiny titans

I'LL TAKE THREE CHOCOLATE FROSTED, FOUR GLAZED WITH SPRINKLES, TWO CINNAMON TWISTS, AND FIVE JELLY DONUTS PLEASE.

COACH

OH, AND ONE CAFFÉ LATTE ESPRESSO... WITH LOWFAT MILK.

I'M ON A DIET!

I'LL HAVE THE SAME.

CYBORG

STARFIRE

RAVEN

KID FLASH

MISS MARTIAN

MAMMOTH

TERRA

BEAST BOY

ROBIN

WONDER GIRL

BUMBLEBEE

JERICHO

ROSE

SPEEDY

YER RIGHT, COACH LOBO, THAT COFFEE GUY'S A HOOT!
COACH
tiny titans
YEAH, HE SURE POURS A MEAN CUP O' JOE!
CLINK!
COACH

SIP
OOPS.
COACH

SEE YA LATER, BOSSMAN!
COACH

BBZZZZ

MEANWHILE...
BBZZZZ

LUNCHROOM!
MR. DARKSEID, MAY I SEE YOU IN MY OFFICE FOR A MOMENT?
YES, SIR!

MINUTES LATER...
YOU WANTED TO SEE ME, SIR?
YES, DARKSEID.
I HAVE A SPECIAL JOB FOR YOU.
IT SEEMS SOMEONE HAS LEFT A MESS IN OUR SCHOOL.

DO YOU NEED ME TO BE ACTING PRINCIPAL FOR THE DAY ONCE AGAIN, SIR?

NO. NOT QUITE.
I NEED YOU TO BE...

JANITOR FOR THE DAY!

WHAT'S WRONG, DARKSEID?

DON'T I GET A JACKET THIS TIME?

OH, RIGHT! HERE YOU GO!

SLEEVE

BUTTON
DARKSEID

CAP

DARKSEID
LET'S DO THIS!

OH, BY THE WAY, I PREFER THE TITLE MAINTENANCE ENGINEER.
ALL RIGHT THEN. YOU COULD START WITH THE COFFEE SPILL IN THE HALLWAY.
MR. MAINTENANCE ENGINEER.

—BUCKET!

SIDEKICK
ELEMENT
tiny titans

SIDEKICK CITY
ELEMENTARY
DARK

SLOSH
SLOP

SIDEKICK CITY
ELEMENTARY

HEY!
COME BACK HERE!
NYAH!
NYAH NYAH!

PRINCIPAL SLADE'S

STOP!
I, DARKSEID, COMMAND THEE!

WHAT IS THE PROBLEM?

THEY TOOK MY UTILITY BELT AND MESSED UP MY HAIR!
NO, WE DIDN'T.
DID TOO!
I DON'T KNOW WHAT BIRD BOY IS TALKING ABOUT!
PRINCIPAL SLADE'S OFFICE

SILENCE!
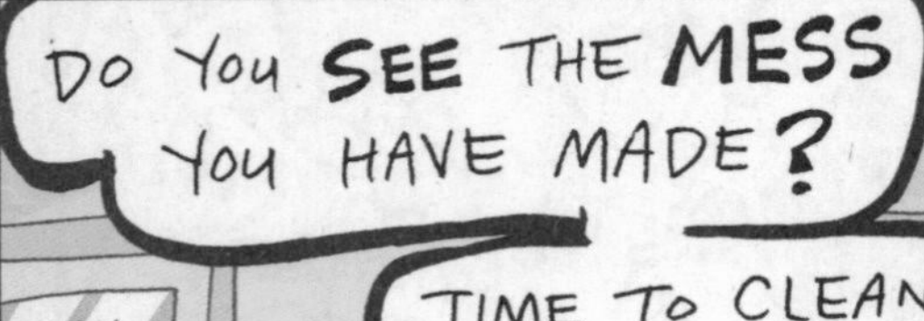
DO YOU SEE THE MESS YOU HAVE MADE?

TIME TO CLEAN IT UP...
PRINCIPAL SLADE'S OFFICE

...IN DETENTION!
WHAT?
YOU CAN'T!

OH YEAH?
I WAS ONCE PRINCIPAL OF THIS SCHOOL!
ONLY FOR A DAY.

SIDEKICK CI
ELEMENTA

IT STILL COUNTS!

GO.

SIDEKICK C
ELEMENT

DARKSEID HAS SPOKEN!

tiny titans

WELCOME DETENTION

THIS IS ALL YOUR FAULT, WONDER BOY!

NO, IT'S NOT! YOU GUYS ARE THE ONES WHO TOOK MY STUFF!

IT'S YOUR FAULT THAT WE ARE HERE! I SHOULDN'T EVEN BE HERE TODAY!

OH, IS THAT RIGHT?

AND I SHOULD BE BATMAN'S PARTNER!

HEY!
NO TALKING!
YOU BOYS JUST BOUGHT YOURSELVES ONE MORE DAY OF DETENTION!
DETENTION

AW MAN!
THAT'S NOT FAIR!

THAT'S IT! YOU JUST GOT ANOTHER DAY!

HUH?

ANOTHER DAY!

BUT... I...

KEEP TALKING AND YOU'LL FIND YOURSELVES SITTING WITH THOSE GUYS!

THOSE GUYS ARE ALWAYS HERE!

I LIKE CLAY.

—WHAT THE?

MR. DARKSEID?
I'M HERE TO CHECK YOUR LIGHTBULBS.
tiny titans

UH... KROC?

THROW!

SMASH
DARKSEID

BOY! IT SURE TURNED INTO ONE OF THE BLACKEST NIGHTS!

DO YOU HAVE ANY LANTERNS IN YOUR TOOLBOX?
CLICK!

MAYBE A GREEN ONE?
LET'S SEE... ORANGE, RED, YELLOW, INDIGO... NOPE, NO GREEN ONES.
WE'LL HAVE TO STICK WITH THE FLASHLIGHTS.
-GREEN!

ATTENTION STUDENTS! TODAY'S DETENTION SESSION IS COMING TO AN END!
DUELA, YOUR DAD IS HERE TO PICK YOU UP!
tiny titans

BYE, BYE, ROBBIE! MWAH! SEE YA TOMORROW!

UNGH...
HA HA! SHE LIKES YOU!

MINUTES LATER...
ENIGMA! YOUR DAD IS HERE TO PICK YOU UP!

BYE, ROBBIE! MWAH!
SEE YA LATER!

—YES COMMISSIONER!

tiny titans
HERE'S YOUR COFFEE, MONITOR.
THANKS, ANTI-MONITOR.
DID YOU GET IT HOW I LIKE IT?
OF COURSE.
I GOT IT EXACTLY THE WAY I LIKE IT BUT OPPOSITE.
CREAM AND SUGAR?
NOPE. SUGAR AND CREAM.
BUT I WANTED CREAM AND SUGAR!
I KNOW. THAT'S WHAT I GOT.
ONLY OPPOSITE.
I KNOW YOU KNOW! BUT THAT'S NOT WHAT I WANTED!
YES, IT IS.
NO, IT'S NOT!
YES, IT IS.
HOW DO YOU KNOW?
BECAUSE, IT'S OPPOSITE OF WHAT I WANTED.
ALL RIGHT! ALL RIGHT! I'LL DRINK IT!
SIP!

SPIT!
AHK!
THIS IS COLD!
THAT'S TRUE.
IT'S COLD BECAUSE I LIKE MINE HOT.
I LIKE HOT COFFEE, TOO!
OH, WAIT. YOU WANTED COFFEE?
HUH?
THEN WHAT'S THIS?
THE OPPOSITE.
THE OPPOSITE OF WHAT?
COFFEE.
WHAT'S THE OPPOSITE OF COFFEE?
THE STUFF YOU'RE DRINKING.
AAHHGG!!

SIP.

MMM, IT'S GOOD THIS WAY, TOO! NO WONDER HE HATED IT!

LATER, KID.

YOU'RE STILL HERE?
YEP. I'M WAITING FOR THE DARK KNIGHT.

DARK KNIGHT?
DON'T YOU MEAN BLACKEST NIGHT?

No, it's DARK KNIGHT.
As in BATMAN: THE DARK KNIGHT. They call him that sometimes.
Oh, okay.
SLOP
SLOSH

So, does he have a GREEN LANTERN?
No. Just a utility belt.

Okay, Robin.
See ya in the morning.
DARKSEID

CLICK!

Blackest night indeed.

–DYNAMIC!

tiny titans presents... the Kroc files

AW YEAH JOKE TIME!
WHY DID THE COOKIE GO TO THE DOCTOR?
WHY?
HE WAS FEELING CRUMBY!
WHAT DID ONE VOLCANO SAY TO THE OTHER VOLCANO?
WHAT?
DO YOU LAVA ME?
I LAVA LOLLIPOP!
WHAT DO YOU GIVE A 300-POUND GORILLA FOR HIS BIRTHDAY?
WHAT?
I DON'T KNOW, BUT YOU BETTER HOPE HE LIKES IT!
SHE'S RIGHT, Y'KNOW.
WHAT DID ONE DOVE SAY TO THE OTHER DOVE?
WHAT?
I DOVE YOU!
BEAST BOY?
COO COO!
-DONE.

Class Photos

AQUALAD
AND FLUFFY
BEAST BOY
CYBORG

KID DEVIL
AAHH-CHOOo!
FOOSH!
KID FLASH
MISS MARTIAN

RAVEN
SPEEDY
TRICK ARROWS
STARFIRE
WONDER GIRL